a Call Home

VANESSA GODDARD

ISBN
978-1-959314-40-0 (Paperback)
978-1-959314-41-7 (eBook)

Table of Contents

Introduction

What would you do if God blessed you with a vision of your future? An actual vision that was very specific in nature. This vision would only glorify His good works in this world. Would it matter if it was one of great joy or one of great sorrow? What would you do in the coming years until the fulfillment of this vision? What would you think knowing just a glimpse of the future?

It is my belief that our hopes and faith are what dreams are made of. We all have dreams for our own lives and for the lives of our children, who have their own ideas.

I have had my own. Life has not always turned out the way I had hoped for. Life is funny that way when we alone are in control.

But to tell the truth, I am at peace now and have been for many years— at peace with who I am and what I am in Christ Jesus. By His strength and grace peace fills my life. I know I'm on the right track with God's will for me. For you see, God has His own plans for me and for my children to become all they can be in Him who made us for His glory.

I urge you to find and experience God's peace in your life and be at peace.

The STORY behind the STORY

Why did I write this book?

Some years ago I suffered with this ailment that afflicts most parents, the Empty-Nest Syndrome. Soon after my last son left my home to be on his own. I had an overwhelming feeling of loneliness and found myself wandering through my house sort of aimlessly, not knowing what to do.

I kept looking for something to do which isn't easy in a small house. Cleaning was easy and didn't take much time. I'd already done all the updates I could do on my house as well as all the painting. And I didn't have any other refinishing projects in the garage to work on.

I'm a Christian, believer in God Almighty and that Jesus was and is His only Son who came to save me from my sins as well as everyone else who would accept this truth and believe.

I went to a workshop hosted by my church that was to search for what purpose God would have me do now. As they said, "Everyone ends up somewhere, but few end up somewhere on purpose"

I had an inspiration soon after that so I decided to put pen to paper (so to speak). To make a long story short, I ended up writing a complete manuscript. I searched the web to see who I might be able to submit it to just to see if it was good enough to be published.

In less than 2 months I received a call from Tate Publishing offering me a contract to do just that. I was amazed to say the least. Li'l, old me, who never ever thought about writing a book before was going to be published.

There was a lot of work ahead for the next year. But through God's inspiration and my devotion that book has now been published. And what a success it has been thus far.

I have sold some copies to friends and family who wanted to purchase it. The stories they have told me of how it touched their lives in some way is exciting to hear. In fact, they past it on to someone else they knew for that same reason, to touch their life also. What more could you ask for in success. God is touching lives where I could not.

I laughed, I cried, and I prayed as I read 'A Call Home'. It's an emotional roller coaster that overwhelms the senses. Vanessa Goddard reveals herself as a master storyteller, weaving an intricate pattern on every page. Find joy in your children as you hold them close, praise God for His guidance, and remember all that is good in this life.

REVIEWED BY

Donna McCartney, Author

A Call Home is an emotionally charged story of a single mom and her family that have been united in tragedy. It tells of their life events throughout have made them a strong Christian family to always be there for one another.

GOD inspired me to write this book when I was suffering from the empty-nest syndrome and was desperately seeking something to do. When God inspires, it doesn't take long to do something. Writing this book was easy as I prayed each morning what to write. It just flowed to write of some of the things I remember.

Although this is a fictional story to me it is not for everyone. It has touched readers in a way they feel they must share it with someone else and, have thus, passed it on.

The cover is a life saving light that calls for all to come home. Home is filled with love, comfort, and joy (most of the time).

Chapter 1

"Well, now what? I've done everything I can think of," I said aloud as I look around. "Haven't I?"

"What about that? You can see if that fits."

"No., I have already"

"Umm... Well... Let's see. Let me think... " I spotted a smaller blade, "How about that?"

"No," I sighed, remembering I'd already tried that too. "Huh. I try and try and try I just can't get it no matter how hard I try. Well, I guess that's that then. I don't know why I try so hard to be such a perfectionist when it comes to things like this."

"Talking to yourself again I see?"

Startled, I looked up, my mouth open as if to say something when I saw that cheshire grin. He had it down pact for a long time now. Just one of those things that came naturally.

Of course I didn't have to ask how long he had been standing there leaning against the doorway. I could see it in his eyes. Those beautiful brown, sparkling eyes laughing at me yet once again. I knew he had been there long enough to hear the whole conversation.

Well, at least part of it. He caught me, again. No use trying to deny it then. It does seem, though; he had a habit of sneaking up on me to do just that. And always when I'm so focused.

He stood there in the open doorway just looking at me, silhouetted in the setting sun, laughing. His high cheek bones almost touching his eyes highlighted the glimmer of his silent laughter. I couldn't help but think of how handsome this boy was with the light fading behind him. I had to smile.

"No. Actually I'm talking with God." I said quite seriously.

"Did He answer this time?" he asked with a sarcastic chuckle.

"He always talks to me... " I stopped mid-sentence about to say something else when I remembered we had something to do tonight. "What time is it anyway?" I asked as I realized how late it must be for him to come in. I'm sure my eyes were as big as bugs.

"That's why I'm here" he said politely. "We're gonna be late if you don't pack it in for the night." he said chuckling as he turned to walk away.

"Where's your brothers?" I yelled after him.

He stopped and poked his head around the corner, "They're on the Play Station, what else?"

"They're ready to go then?" I had to queried, knowing better.

"What do you think?" he yelled back as he walked off.

"All right, all right, I'm coming," I said as I quickly headed for the door wiping my hands on my pants to get some of the dust off.. I couldn't help but notice how he walked as I closed and locked the door.

The sun was low in the sky as I watch him from behind, walking to the house. His stride was long and almost cocky the way he walked. It was as if to say he knew I was watching him and he had to strut his li'l ole stuff. All teenagers did that, mine did anyway. They all new just how handsome they were. All the girls had to hang around them. Something I wish I could rectify. Maybe they wouldn't have such an inflated ego when it came to their looks. If only that were possible. But they did love the attention.

Kyle, middle of the three, was the worst of them. He's had girls of all ages, younger and older, hanging all over him even before he was a teenager. Blonde hair and blue, twinkling eyes with a deep, sultry voice. The combination had everyone believing he was much older and mature than he actually was. A take charge kind of person. At five, ten he had a well toned, muscular build the girls couldn't keep their hands off of.

He told me once that it was all my fault, of course, that the older kids thought he was their age. The conversations we've had over the years. Kyle is right. He had matured faster in some ways. I don't believe in lying or suppressing the truth from any of my boys. They have the right to know the truth about things if they want to know. Imagine that, talking to your children can help them mature faster.

Of course, some things truly needed to be put on hold depending on their age. But for the most part, all they had to do is ask. And they knew it. Kyle asked a lot of questions.

Nathaniel, my baby, was heading directly in Kyle's footsteps. He discovered early just how much he liked being around the older kids. He figured out that by hanging around Kyle he could do almost everything his brother did. That's when they let him tag along of course. Those were also the times they forgot that he was younger and shouldn't always be with them.

Nat could almost pass for Kyle's twin though. If it weren't for two years and his brown, ornery eyes they would be. Nat was born with those eyes. That meant trouble. I could see if from the beginning.

They both took more after the father than me though. Good looking and full of trouble. The one thing they all had in common was a very bad case of me-itis.

Jeremy was different, in looks anyway. He took more after my side than his dad's. He was taller than his brothers, quickly approaching the six foot his granddad was. He also had the brown hair, brown eyes and, of course, the high cheekbones like me. The Cheshire grin and the confident strut came with years of practice.

He still had *me*-itis like his brothers but it wasn't quite as bad. What kid didn't? He also had a very giving heart for others, always wanting to help his friends. They all were extremely handsome and they knew it. And they used their good looks every chance they got.

"Put up the game and get ready, it's time to get going" I yelled at Nat and Kyle as I walked into the house. I was heading for my room for a quick change when I heard "But we're not done yet." I stopped in the hall and looked back in the direction from which the voice came, "Do we really have to grow through this again? It's time and you know it. So why do you think you can give me problems?"

Silence. "You got five minutes to get ready and get out to the car. That's it!" I paused, "And no more out of the peanut gallery." I had to add for good measure before continuing to my room.

Good I thought as I changed. *Maybe tonight I can actually enjoy my meal instead of hurrying it down because we got to church late again. Trying to sing on a full stomach is bad for you. And we were rehearsing the Easter special tonight.*

The only sounds coming from outside my room were the three boys scuffling out of the house to get to the car. Halleluiah, no arguments. We were going to have a good evening.

And the evening was great. We had a good meal. The ladies made tacos tonight with all the trimmings along with refried beans and Spanish rice.

We had good company at our table, too. A new couple that joined the church just last Sunday. Emily and Brice were young, newlywed just six months ago. They were anxious to have kids, like all young couples, but felt they should wait for a little while. They wanted to chance to learn how to live together first.

I agreed. Getting married is quite an adjustment in itself. They needed the time to enjoy each other before the kids came and changed everything. That's a whole other Chapter to married life.

Once dinner was done, Emily and Brice went off to one of the side rooms for the prayer meeting. I asked if they would mind putting us in prayer they left. Raising three teenage boys alone was exhausting at times. And our situation was going to be changing somewhat this summer. Their dad was getting out of jail and expecting only God knows what. I hadn't talked to him for a while and I didn't want to.

Besides, I truly was too busy to visit. Refinishing antiques was not easy and very time consuming. You had to be patient and meticulous not to damage the old wood when you're trying to restore it. At least as close to its original condition as humanly possible. There was a lot of work involved in the whole process.

Emily said they would have our family added to the prayer list. I headed up to choir practice since the boys had already taken off for the youth group. We were going to be a part of the resurrection story on Easter Sunday. Tonight was the first dress rehearsal with all the others involved, so it was an important one. We only had about a month before it was time to perform. And then we had regular choir to rehearse for next Sunday. It was going to be a busy night.

Everyone had finally gathered to start choir rehearsal. We were just getting started when I heard someone whispering 'mom' from behind me. I quickly dismissed it. The boys knew they shouldn't be here. I opened my mouth to sing but no sound came out. I heard 'mom' whispered again. I looked back, yet I didn't see anyone. There was only darkness. I shut my eyes, took a deep breath and... There it was again.

Chapter **2**

On the ride home after church the boys were talking a mile a minute as they usually did. Especially when they were excited about something. This time it was about the youth group rafting trip this weekend. The rapids were about fifty miles away beautifully nestled at the base of the mountains.

They talked about what to wear and what to take, which wasn't much. And, let's not forget the most important thing, who they were going to sit next to.

Now that was an interesting conversation to hear. Kyle and Nat ran down a list of names of the girls they liked and wanted to sit next to. It was all quite funny when you stop to think about it. At least it was until one of them brought up Tess.

Jeremy and Tess had been more or less a couple for a long time now. I sometimes hate to think of how long that has actually been. They're relationship had grown extensively over this past year or so. We had several discussions over the seriousness that was apparent.

But Tess was definitely good for him and he was good for her, so her parents tell me. They spent as much of their waking hours as possible with each other. Mostly just exchanging their own hopes and dreams.

Kyle has seemed to set his eyes on someone new. Jackie, I think he said her name was. Long dark hair and legs that went on forever, if you can believe him. I haven't met her yet but I'm sure I will soon enough. The bus was leaving at eight a.m. sharp Saturday morning.

Nathaniel couldn't seem to make up his mind from what I heard coming from the back seat of my ghetto van, as the boys aptly named it. But Nat sounded like he just wants to sit in the middle of all of them in his raft. I wonder if he really thinks it's going to happen that way. Oh well, time will tell.

As we pulled into the drive Jeremy leaned over to whisper in my ear, "I need to talk to you in private." I looked over my shoulder so I could look into his eyes knowing instantly that this was something serious.

Nat and Kyle bolted out of the van trying to be the first at the front door before I even shut off the engine. "Get ready for bed." I yelled out the window after them.

"Ah," I heard as I turned back to face Jeremy. "We'll talk inside" I said as we got out of the van to head for the door when I told Nat and Kyle to get ready for bed again when it started.

"But mom, it's too early. Can't we play a game first?" Nat said while waiting at the door for me to get there. Both Nat and Kyle looked at me with that mastered puppy dog look. "Not tonight!" I said immediately. "Please, please, please" they begged. "Not tonight!" I repeated, my voice rising half an octave.

I can get so agitated when they want something and have to keep asking till I finally give in. Or get mad because they just won't quit and I really have had enough. Thankfully they realized by my tone this was not the night to push it.

Once inside the boys retreated to their rooms while I went to put my things away. As I was walking to Jeremy's room I thought I heard someone whisper "mom" again. I stopped at Kyle's room, he was talking to someone on the phone I gathered by what I heard from behind his closed door.

I took a step across the hall to listen at Nat's door. All I heard there was his music. I guess he'd decided to practice his keyboard for a bit before bed. Well, he did have a lesson tomorrow so I guess it was alright.

I stopped at Jeremy's room and knocked on the open door. He was sitting on the bed waiting for me. I also noticed that he was fiddling with something in his hands.

When he heard me he quickly put his hand behind his back as he looked up. He asked me to shut the door so we could talk alone.

As I shut the door I said, "This sounds so serious. So, what's going on, kiddo?" I sat down at the foot of the bed as I usually do, looking directly at him. His eyes met mine, "I wanted to know... " he paused.

"What?" already feeling like I knew where this was heading.

His eyes were sparkling when he reached behind him to retrieve the secret he had hidden when I came into the room. He waited till I glanced down at his enormous hands before slowly opening them to reveal a small gift box.

I could feel him still looking at me when he opened the box to gauge my reaction. Needless to say, I wasn't at all that surprised. We had talked many, many times the past several months about it.

"Oh, my" I said as I gazed at the elegance. "So, you've decided?" I asked looking up at him.

"Yeah" he said taking a deep, nervous breath, "This weekend. What do you think?"

"I think," then paused, my gaze returning to the small beautiful single diamond engagement ring.. I knew what I said and how I say it now is so very important. But I had questions first. The same questions I'd asked since the first time he told me he wanted to marry Tess.

"School? You've still got a year left and Tess is going off to the university next fall." I looked up from the ring to meet his eyes. "I know, I know. None of that is going to change, mom. Don't worry, we're gonna keep to the plan." Jeremy insisted.

"Jeremy, you know I love Tess half to death. She's a great girl and I believe you two are so good together. But, don't you think it might be a little too soon to be asking."

"No."

"Why?"

"I want her to know that even when she goes away that I still love her and always will. And I want to know that she'll still love me when we're apart."

"But... "

"I know what you're going to ask, mom. And yes, I have prayed excessively about it. I know she's the one God has chosen for me. And I truly believe the answer is yes!" Jeremy looked me straight in the eye before adding, "This is the right time to promise each to the other."

"Are you sure or is it because she'll be leaving soon?" I had to ask. I am his mom.

"Well, yes I'm being selfish. I want the whole world to know how much I love Tess and won't let anyone mess with her while she's away."

"And, pre tell, how are you going to do that?"

"I'm gonna talked to her every night and if she tells me somebody is bothering her, I'll just go up there and take care of business. It's just that simple" he said with confidence.

I laughed. "You don't think that might be a little drastic? She's gonna be a hundred miles away." But I knew that when he sounded that confident, nothing was going to stand in his way. Not even me.

He just winked at me.

"Jeremy, my dear son," I paused so I could put the serious look back on my face, "are you scared of what might happen when she's so far from you?"

He didn't say anything, he just looked at me. Yet there was that twinge of anxiety in his eyes.

"Aha! The eyes tell the truth. That's it, isn't it?" I announced.

"Mom, what if something or someone did happen? What am I gonna do? I love Tess so much it hurts to be without her, even now." Tears started to glisten in his eyes. You could see the fear of losing the best thing in his life. Tess had been his best friend for years. The worry of possibly losing her Well, that's only human.

My heart broke for him. I sighed and put my hand over his, "Honey, you know whatever God brings together no one can tear apart." Such wise words of wisdom, I truly wish they were from me.

"I know you're right, mom. But still... "

"And it's not the time to be worrying about such things that have not happened yet" I said sternly. "I love you very much and I think that if you are absolutely, positively, sure that this is the right time, then, I guess, you have my blessing." I said, smiling. Hoping that would suffice for my blessing.

His expression changed in an instant. His smile lit up the whole room. It probably lit up the whole sky...

'Mom" someone whispered.

I turned to look at the door, "Who is it and what do you want?" I asked anxiously annoyed that one of the boys would be interrupting. No answer. I looked back at Jeremy. He was smiling as he said, "It's time mom."

"Time?" I asked confused. "Time for bed is what it is. Goodnight, love, sweet dreams." I stood up and leaned over to kiss him on the forehead then turned to leave.

'Mom' again the whisper but a little louder this time.

I yanked open the door to discover there was no one there, only darkness. I could have sworn I heard someone calling me. Yet, I'm not sure which one did.

'Mom' They weren't whispering. It was almost like they're yelling now. But who is it? Where are they?

"Mom! Wake up!" someone yelled loudly in my ear.

Chapter 3

My mind seemed cloudy as I struggled against something. I kept blinking, the light was blinding. I was shaking my head from side to side trying to focus on things around me. Then I saw an antique desk in the left corner of the room. I stopped to focus on it. I recognized it. That was the desk given to me by a friend after I had refinished it for her.

My eyes wandered as I turned my head to the other side of the room. Looking to the right I saw a mirrored dresser with a book and other knick knacks on it. That was my dresser. My bible lay right where I put it last night.

In the reflection of the mirror I saw something. A figure was sitting on the edge of my bed. The haze was starting to fade. I must be in my bed for this is my room. I slowly turned to look at the face that had been reflected in the mirror, fear welling in the pit of my stomach. It was Kyle.

"What are you doing here?" I asked sitting up I was still confused at my surroundings. I could have sworn I was just talking to Jeremy in his room. When did I come to bed? I don't remember even saying 'Good night' to Kyle and Nat. I just sat there staring at Kyle. He looked different, his eyes were sad. They were heavy and red like he had been crying.

My lips started to quiver, my eyes were tearing up. I know why he's here. I couldn't stop it. I started crying as I leaned forward into his arms. I realized it all had been a dream.

"Mom," he said softly. His arms wrapped around me tightly as though he thought I might fall. Such strength, such comfort— these were his blessings for me.

"A dream, it was only a dream" my voice was trembling as I spoke. The night Jeremy told me he was absolutely sure he wanted to marry Tess. And had planned on asking her that weekend.

Kyle held me just a little bit tighter when I felt his shoulders starting to shake. It seems he couldn't hold back his own tears either. So we sat there in each other's arms, crying.

Kyle finally broke the silence, "Colin called. He said he'd be here within the hour. He's driving in. I was going to let you try to sleep a little longer but Mandy was scratching at your door." We looked down at Mandy when she let out a bark. "I think she knew something was up. I tried to get her to go outside. She wouldn't go. She just kept scratching your door to come in. That's when I heard you."

Good old Mandy, my seven year old, forty pound, brown and red Irish setter. She was a rescue pup and had the sweetest, most gentle personality any dog could ever have. She always knew when something was bothering me and she needed to be close. But, oh, so protective. She would even growl at the boys if they dared to talk cross to me. She was their reminder to always be respectful.

She was sitting right next to me on the floor. Her tail was wagging as she let out another loud bark. That was her way of asking to get next to me. So I patted the bed on the other side and up she jumped. She had to walk all over me to get to the other side. Circling a couple of times on the bed, she finally settled down with her head on my lap. She looked up at me with soulful eyes as I reached to pet her.

My mind was whispering 'help'. I had to get myself together. Today was going to be a very, very long day. So many things to do before...

"Mandy, you ready to go outside?" I asked. She immediately got up and jump off the bed to head for the door. Before she reached it she turned and started barking at Kyle and me. "I guess it's time to get up and get going," I said as Kyle stood up so I could get out of bed. I moved slowly. The stiffness made my body ache all over. I stood up and started swaying. I put out my hand for something to grab to catch my balance myself. Kyle grabbed it immediately to steady me.

"Whoa, there mom. You OK?" concern dripping through his voice and showing on his face.

"Yeah, I'm fine. Just moved a little too fast. I'm OK." I stood there another couple of seconds to let the stiffness seep from my body. I took a deep breath before I tried to move again. "I don't suppose you have coffee, do you?" I looked at Kyle with wide, pleading eyes.

"It's started."

"So... did you get any sleep?" I asked, concerned myself he didn't get much.

"Yeah. Some, you know, off and on. But every time I closed my eyes, my mind wouldn't shut up." He took a deep breath, it sounded like a sigh.

"I know the feeling." I agreed.

Mandy started barking at us from the door, waiting for one of us to let her out back.

"Go on, let her out. I'll be right there." I said trying to gain some composure.

Kyle told Mandy to 'Come' as he walked passed her. She headed out the door down the hall. I didn't start moving again until I heard the back door open and close. I grabbed my robe and put it on as I headed for the kitchen.

I could hear Kyle getting the cups out of the cupboard as I made my way down the hall. I was feeling a better now that I was moving. I wasn't quite as stiff as before. As I entered the kitchen, Kyle was pouring the coffee. I backed up a step or two to sit down at the dining table. There wasn't room in my kitchen to put it. Obviously it was too small.

"Here you go," he said as he put the hot cup of coffee in front of me. "You know we got plenty of time, so there's no hurry in anything today?" he said. I could still hear the concern in his voice.

I waited for Kyle to join me before I stated the obvious. "I dreamed about him last night. I can't stop thinking about him, all of us growing up here in this house."

"Mom, it's our home. That's what you made it every day of our lives" he said reassuredly.

"Good and bad?" I asked with all the half heartedness I could muster.

"Well, of course. You can't have the good without the bad, right? Something I seem to remember you told us a lot." There was a smirk on his face.

"That's how a family grows." And I thanked God for the strength our family had. Every day I had to praise Him for this truth.

"I know. You were like a broken record growing up." We both laughed. How many times had I used that line?

"Well, if you kids hadn't become brain-dead and developed that horrible case of *me*-itis, I wouldn't have sounded like a broken record, now would I?"

"Yeah, yeah, yeah." We both chuckled at the too numerous of times to count we had gone through the same things, over and over and over again.

"You think it's true?" Kyle asked.

"What?"

"What you say about your work. Is that really how you think God works in us?"

"Yes, I do." I said quietly. I remember the story well that I've told them on more than one occasion. I started to recount the first time I brought home one of my first projects.

Chapter 4

"All right, set it down easy."

Jeremy and Kyle were carrying in a wooden bookcase headboard of the twin bed frame I had just acquired. Nat was carrying the footboard and I had both side rails. Nat was the only one struggling with his piece of furniture. I told him I thought it was too heavy for him, but he insisted. He couldn't be left out.

Bang! We heard all of the sudden. Nat let the footboard drop just barely missing his foot when it hit the floor. Then it fell over on its side. He looked up at me with a half smile and one eye squinted, "Sorry" he said contritely.

"Heh! Mom said 'put it down' not 'drop it'" Jeremy said angrily as he and Kyle set their piece down.

That started it. Jeremy and Kyle had started in on the poor little guy for being careless. Telling him he could have hurt one of them even though he wasn't that close.

In essence, they were making him feel worse than he already did.

"That's enough you two," I broke in with enough force to stop any more badgering of their brother. "It didn't break and no one got hurt." I said as I walked over to Nat and put my hand on his shoulder. "And Kyle, you looked like you were having a bit of trouble yourself." I said quizzically meeting his defiant gaze.

"Yeah!" Jeremy butted in. "I was carrying this heavy thing all by myself practically. You were just guiding it." He paused just a split second before adding, "Maybe." He just had to continue with the harassment.

"Was not. I was carrying it too." Kyle yelled. He wasn't going to get blamed for not doing something again.

"Well, I was carrying this all by myself" Nat said defiantly. "So there!" And he stuck out his tongue at his brothers as if to say that he's the one that did a better job.

"Alright, alright. That's enough!" It was time to break this up before it got to be an ugly yelling match. Time to change tactics. "It's time for lunch, who's hungry?"

"I am" all three of them yelled at once.

"Then let's get something to eat." We all headed out the door of my soon to be workshop and into the house for sandwiches. Walking back to the house I could see the three still at it, poking at each other.

Nat suddenly stopped and turned around, "Mom, can I help you?" he asked excitedly.

"With lunch? Sure." I said, pleased he would ask.

"No, with that" he said pointing back to the building we just left.

"You mean, you want to help refinish the bed?" knowing what he really meant the first time he asked.

"Yeah. Please, please, please" be begged.

"Sure, if you want to. But no power tools" I said sternly.

"Ah... " he was crushed, "why not?"

"Because five year olds don't use power tools" I answered as I poked my finger on the tip of his nose. "And neither do you so don't even ask." I had to add when Jeremy and Kyle turned around too.

You could see the excitement fade from their eyes when I said that. I had to smile at the look on those little faces. But I did like their help with things and they seemed eager. But only with the things they wanted to help with. There was only so much little ones could do.

If only their attention span would last more than a few minutes it could be done right the first time Then I wouldn't have to go back over it.

Back in the house, the boys went to wash up while I prepared their favorite sandwich of the year, peanut butter and jelly with a side of pretzels and a cup of milk. I could hear them chattering and fussing about who was going to be first to wash, then rushing back to get what they claimed to be the best seat at the table. Of course, Jeremy won. The biggest always wins.

I brought in the sandwiches on paper plates with the bag of pretzels to be dished out at the table. I set one plate in front of each boy then went back for the milk. I went to get mine after prayer and they started eating. When I sat down Jeremy asked, "How long is it gonna take you to refinish the bed, mom?"

"I don't know, a week or two. Maybe longer."

"That's a long time." Kyle said. I laughed.

"Why?" asked Nat. He was chewing a mouthful of food with his elbows on the table and swinging his feet under the table. One look from me and he removed his elbows from the table.

"Well, because there's a lot to do to get the bed ready to use again."

"It's ready, it's not broken." Nat interrupted.

Jeremy, of course, had to add his two cents worth, "It's ugly, dummy" he said sarcastically.

"I'm not a dummy!" Nat tried to yell at the top of his lungs. But he had a mouthful of food. It went flying everywhere. Everyone broke into hysterical laughter at the sight. Kyle almost fell out of his chair he was laughing so hard. Nat finished with the food in his mouth and yelled again, "I'm not a dummy!"

"Jeremy" I berated, trying desperately to hold my own laughter.

"Nat, Jeremy's right. It is ugly. It's had a lot of use obviously" I said trying to turn this around from a side show. "It's been used so much so that the paint's coming off. The people that owned it didn't take very good care of it. I guess that's why they were going to throw it away. They couldn't see any more use in it."

"Yeah, it looks like trash." Kyle said between bites.

"Yeah, but they didn't know that real beauty lies beneath the surface" I said quickly. "There's a lot of work to be done before it looks good again. And it can be dangerous if you don't know what you're doing."

"What can be dangerous about cleaning up an old bed?" Jeremy asked.

"Because, honey, I don't just clean it up. I work very hard at making it look good again. I have stripping chemicals and tools in my workshop. And they can be very dangerous if you don't know how to use them. In fact, I'm still learning. That's why none of you are allowed in there without me. I also want to make sure that it will stand up to whatever you kids can dish out on it." I managed to get it all in between bites of my sandwich.

Jeremy, Kyle, and Nat just sat there eating their peanut butter and jelly listening to what I was saying. At least for now I had their attention. I decided to keep going while they were listening.

"So, after I clean up all that gunky stuff that's on it I can start stripping it down to get the paint off."

"Why not just re-paint it? It'd be a lot easier." Jeremy, the wise, asked.

"Yeah, it would be easier" I agreed. "But I'm particular about how I want that bed to look. I can see it already. It'll look almost new again when I'm done. But it will take some time."

"I still don't see why we can't help?" Nat asked as he gulped down the rest of his milk.

"Baby, you can help just not with the chemicals I use to strip the paint off. It can hurt you if it gets on your skin. It will burn" showing my concern over their well being.

Jeremy opened his mouth to say something but I put up my hand to shush him before he could.

"That's not all I have to do. So now I already have two different ways that it needs to be cleaned. And you guys can help with that." I said reassuring them that there was something they could help with. "After all that, I sand it down until the wood is smooth. And that takes more time. When I'm done with all that, I put some other chemical on it that will help protect all the work I've done to make it look beautiful again."

Now's my opportunity. I thought, *What a perfect opening.* They were still listening. Well, at least Jeremy was.

"You know, people sometimes think that way about themselves, too." I said quizzically.

Jeremy asked, "What do you mean?"

"Some people think they are ugly on the inside." I stated matter-of-factly.

"Yeah, only the ugly people." Kyle piped in before he guzzled down the rest of his milk.

"No. The only real ugly is on the inside of people. There are people that have bad things happen in their lives to make them feel ugly. They feel like they are no good anymore just like that bed out there. But God doesn't see them that way. They don't know that there is this loving God who can make them look and feel beautiful again on the inside."

"How can God make ugly people look good?" Nat asked with a so serious look on his face.

"The inside of people is what God sees, not the outside. He takes what is ugly on the inside and works on it very hard to make it look beautiful. Sort of like what I'm going to do with that bed out there. And that takes a lot of time for God to do his work in people. It's not an easy job cleaning us up."

"I don't get it mom. You can't clean the inside of that bed— there isn't any. So how can you and God be doing the same thing?" Jeremy asked and they all laughed. I guess it did sound funny.

"Remember John 3:16? 'for God so loved the world that He gave His only begotten son that whosoever believed in him would not perish but have everlasting life" the quoted the scripture with me.

I continued, "We are all sinners, right? Doesn't matter if you are good looking or not?" I was ecstatic, all three were still listening.

"Yeah" they agreed.

"And we can only be saved by God through belief in his son, Jesus Christ, right?"

"Yeah" they agreed again.

"And when we become saved God changes us from the inside out.

"How?"

"Well... I see God working in each of our lives every day. He does all the scraping and sanding and smoothing to teach us about life. That's all the good times and bad times we have in our lives. And it takes our whole lifetime for God to finish. That's how we learn how to do things God's way. When He's done, we're as beautiful as Jesus/"

I paused only a moment to add the final touch. "That's kinda what I will do with that bed. I'll work on it until it looks beautiful again."

I could see Jeremy's mind working. He was really thinking about it. Maybe something made sense to him. I noticed I already lost Kyle and Nat a little while back when they started having a food fight with the leftover pretzels. I started clearing the table.

"So, maybe if you come out to the workshop once in a while to see what I'm doing it might make more sense. You think?" I asked.

"So... God's gonna finish me off, huh?" Jeremy asked a bit sarcastically. His brothers chiming together in agreement, "Yeah, God's gonna finish you!." We all laughed.

Chapter 5

"Hey, mom. You in there?" Kyle asked to get my attention.

Startled, I blinked a couple of times then looked up at Kyle sitting across from me. "I was just thinking... " There was a sudden knock at the front door. "Has it been an hour already?"

"No," Kyle said. "I called Nat after I talked to Colin. He said he'd come on over. He wants to be here when Colin got in." Kyle was telling me as he headed for the door.

"Hey, bro." Kyle said to his brother as he opened the door for his brother to come in. "Want some coffee? Fresh brewed."

"Nah, I'm good for now. I stopped to get a shot before I came." Nat told Kyle as he walked over to where I was sitting. He leaned down to give me a kiss on the forehead and a hug before sitting down beside me. Kyle took his place across from me. Nat wasn't really a coffee drinker, but he did have shots of espresso once in a while.

"Where's Candy?" I asked.

"She's still sleeping. I'll get her later" Nat said. He took my hand and held it tight—watching, waiting. I squeezed his hand back to let him know everything was OK.

Kyle interrupted, "Mom was just going to tell me what she was so lost in thought about" he giggled. "You should have seen the look on her face. You know the one I mean. That look of 'a million miles away." They both started laughing.

Kyle continued, "I told you we got it from her." We all smiled. Yeah, they only thought that. They all had developed their own look of 'a million miles away'. They picked up more traits from me than I'd like to admit sometimes. At least it wasn't all the bad ones. There was some good ones in the mix.

"Ok," I said as I rubbed my eyes. We heard scratching on the back door. Nat got up and went to the back door. As soon as he opened it Mandy came pouncing in all excited to see him. She jumped up on Nat, her paws on his chest, her hind quarters bouncing as if she was trying to jump up in his arms. It was always a funny sight.

"Down Mandy, down." Nat said as he started to pet her. "That's a good girl." Actually, he was riling her up some more for playtime. He got down on one knee to tousle the top of her head and talking to her as he always did.

We all broke out in laughter when she quickly jumped up on Nat sitting and he fell to the floor. That's all she needed to be all over him. He had to give her some attention before she would settle down, she was so happy to see him.

"All right, down now girl." He commanded. Mandy went over to Kyle next to get a little attention from him before she ended up at my feet. She just had to lay down with her head on top of them.

"I was just thinking about when I started refinishing that twin bed Tami's using. Remember when we first brought it home?" We all chuckled a bit remembering that day.

"Yeah. It looked like a piece junk for the trash man." Kyle said.

"Hey, I remember that. But it was mine in the first place. It should have stayed in my family and not gone somewhere else." Nat protested. I can't hardly blame him though. I know he thought it was special because I fixed it up just for him to use when he was five.

"Hey, you don't got kids." Kyle retorted.

"So, I broke it in. And you never know, someday we might." Nat retorted back.

"That hardly seems likely" Kyle piped.

"Regardless,," I told Nat. "Right now Tami needs it and you don't. You wouldn't want your niece to have to sleep on the floor do you? Besides, I gave you and Candy the table. You use that a whole lot more than you would a twin bed, don't you think?"

"That's right!" Kyle popped out without hesitation. Nat stuck his tongue out in defiance of his brother.

"Anyway, I was just thinking not too long after that, I had this sort of weird type of dream. Yet, it wasn't really a dream, you know. It's that place in-between when you're not really asleep but you aren't really awake either?"

They both nodded. They even looked a little intrigued. Maybe that was my mind playing tricks on me.

"Anyway, in this dream I saw Jeremy. And he was all growed up." I took another drink of coffee and as I sat the cup down I put my elbow on the table to cradle my chin in my hand. Memories. "He was so handsome, like now. Just standing there not saying anything, only silence." I sat quiet for a bit, thinking.

"There was this brilliant light behind him and all around, almost... " I had to pause a moment to collect myself. I felt the tears welling in my eyes and I was really trying not to cry. "I really don't know how to describe it. But when I woke up I couldn't get it out of my head.

I kept thinking about it and what it meant. Did it actually mean something?" I gulped and closed my eyes slowly, then opened them again. Taking a deep breath I continued, "That's when I realized that God had given me a vision for Jeremy, for all of you actually."

I notice them looking at each other then back to me. They were intrigued. Nat spoke first, "So what was it?"

I looked him straight in the eye and said "What you're doing now." We had talked about God's visions before. Last year Nat had a strong conviction God was calling him to evangelize. But how was the question. He told everyone he came in contact with about the good news of Jesus Christ.

He shouldn't have had to ask. When Nat strayed, God brought him back in a fierce way. All the struggles he'd already been through, especially when it came to Candy. That was a stubbornness God was still working on.

"Look what it's taken to get you to where you are now" I said. We all had our memories of that dark time. "It wasn't that long ago that I thought you might not make it. Then God got a hold of you to bring you back to him. Now, he's working on your own personal story."

"Well," Nat said, "as I remember, God had to do some of that with you too."

"Yes, he did! And we've all come a long way. Haven't we?" I looked at Kyle for his agreement. We all had some problems with Candy and couldn't understand their relationship. But throughout the years Nat and Candy have been together, I especially, have seen God working in both their lives and ours. They've been through some awful hard times but they were still together, working to keep things right between them. What a journey they're on, telling everyone they meet about what God was doing.

Kyle agreed. "To tell you the truth, bro, none of us thought you'd make it this long, being from different worlds and all. But it looks like you guys are making it work."

"Thanks" Nat said appreciatively.

Silence. Jeremy, Kyle and Nat all came to accept and know Jesus Christ as their Savior at a very young age. I'm still amazed at the timing as each of them accepted Jesus and their faith. I remembered how I prayed for each of them every night as always. But it wasn't until I truly gave them over to God for his purpose that they became saved. Each one in his own time and my faith grew a little deeper each time.

Chapter 6

We were sitting in the pew listening to the pastor preaching a sermon series on Revelation. Well, I was listening. The boys were drawing while they were sitting there. It was something to do to keep them quiet and awake during the sermons.

He preached on Revelation 14, the Harvest of the Earth. Then on Revelation 15 and the seven plaques. And so on and so on. Today, he was preaching on Revelation 20, the Dead of Judged.

There was something about today that really caught Jeremy's attention. He was sitting beside me today so it was easy to notice what he was doing while listening. He was still drawing, but he was also listening very intently to what the pastor was saying. All those who didn't believe in Jesus and were saved were going to burn in hell.

When the pastor gave the invitation at the end of service Jeremy's took my hand. I looked up into his eyes.

They were watering up when he asked, "Is that true?" in a whisper.

"Is what true?" I whispered too not wanting to bother anyone around us.

"That everyone that doesn't believe in God and are saved are going to burn in hell." It was a question that had him really bothered. Yet, he had been taught that the Bible is God's truth. The concern in those beautiful, and usually sparkly, brown eyes told me he was very upset with this news revealed today.

"Yes, it's true. You know that, honey"

Tears started to roll down his cheeks. "Mom, I don't want anyone in our family to go to hell. It's a horrible place. We got to do something about it" he insisted. Jeremy always did have a soft heart when it came to people in need, especially family.

"Well, the first thing we can do right now, is go up there to the alter and pray for all our family."

He didn't wait to respond. Jeremy just grabbed my hand and stood to make his way to the alter and making sure that I came with him. He didn't ask if I would pray with him. He knew I would.

We got to our knees as soon as we reached the steps of the alter. Jeremy looked at me and asked, "How?"

I told him, "I'll start and then you can join me." He nodded his head in agreement and then wiped the tear away from his face. He put his hands in mine then we closed our eyes.

"Lord, Heavenly Father, we come before you as your humble servants. Ready for your call to your will in our lives. We come to petition for all in our family that has not been saved by your love and grace. We ask you to soften their hearts that their eyes may see you all around them."

"Yes, Lord, yes." I heard Jeremy whisper in agreement.

I continued, "We ask you to soften their hearts that their ears may hear your call."

"Yes, Lord, yes." I heard Jeremy whisper in agreement again.

"We ask you to use us in any way possible that will help them to come to know you in a very personal way." I was almost on the verge of tears myself thinking of what was in store for my own sister and brothers who were not saved. They didn't even want to talk about it.

Suddenly I felt other arms go around me. I didn't look to see who it was. They were silent as I continued to pray.

"We ask for your strength and courage to tell our loved ones the words you want them to hear from us. And if we are not to be your instruments in their salvation, we ask that you put the right people at the right time for them to hear your voice.

"Yes God" Jeremy interrupted, "I don't want them to go to hell. I want them to go to Heaven. Please help them see that you are the only way for all of us to be together." He stopped.

After a short pause before I could continue, another voice intervened also on our behalf. "Oh God, Lord of our lives, maker of all creation. We humbly ask you grant this petition. Your word says that wherever two or more are gathered in your name, you will hear their prayers. You are our Sovereign Lord who knows the hearts of all people. We are at your mercy. Your will be done on earth as it is in Heaven. In your Son's name, the name of Jesus, we pray. Amen."

Jeremy and I both said 'Amen' at the same time. We also heard several other voices say 'Amen' too. Among them were the voices of Kyle and Nat who had joined us sometime during our prayer.

I opened my eyes to see who else had joined us in prayer. It was Brenda and Lee. They both were very good friends of mine and the boys. We did a lot of fellowship together outside of church. You could call them wonderful friends.

We were a huddle mass, three adults and three children. This was one of the biggest group hugs I had ever had. It was so encouraging to have good friends join you in prayer. Knowing I had prayer warriors that also prayed for me and my family was a great relief.

"Feeling better?" I asked Jeremy.

Chapter 7

We were all lost in our own thoughts when Nat finally broke the silence, "You know what" he said. "That coffee does sound pretty good right about now. Anyone want a refill?" he asked as he got up from the table.

"Sure," I said, one cup was never enough.

Mandy lifted her head when Nat got up to go to the kitchen. She lay there at my feet wagging her tail, just waiting. Then she heard it. The wrestling sound of a paper bag like someone was getting into it, Food. Nat was putting food in her bowl. She got up immediately to go get her breakfast.

Nat came back in with my refill and his own cup after he filled Mandy's water bowl too. I sat watching him sip his coffee thinking about just how much he had changed over the years. Not just physically, but emotionally, spiritually.

He didn't look like Kyle's twin anymore. That changed many, many years ago. He had his own distinct features.

The dirty blonde hair and ornery brown eyes were still all his though. Still, he was a handsome young man with a strong physic that matched his defining looks.

Kyle had changed quite a bit too. He was as handsome as ever with his light blonde hair and hazel blue eyes. The scar that ran down the left side of his face didn't distract from that well defined bone structure. In fact, it only added to his character. His resemblance to his dad was more than either of his brothers.

Now he was starting to settle down. He wasn't the wild child anymore. He was dating a divorcee with two small children, a girl and a boy. And everything seemed to be going OK, as far as I knew anyway.

Kyle met her at some sort of concert and, I guess, hit is off right off the bat. After a couple of dates she told him of her divorce and the kids. She had full custody although their dad did have visitation rights. The kids had just come back from spending a few weeks with dad.

We sat there quietly drinking our coffee. Only God knows what thoughts and memories were going thru their minds. I had my own memories fading in and out. I closed my eyes and took a deep breath again. *I'm doing a lot of that lately*, I thought.

No one was talking when I interrupted, "Well, I think I'll take a shower before Colin gets here." I said as I got up. My cup in hand I headed for my room. Mandy was at my heels, of course. She went everywhere I did.

Before I reached the door Kyle yelled, "Do you want something to eat?" I stopped long enough to say 'no' and let Mandy go in the room ahead of me, "But go ahead if you are." I yelled back and shut the door behind me.

I had to get away. Tears were stinging my eyes again. I didn't want the boys to see me cry. That would have just ended up with all of us crying instead of getting ready.

I went straight to the bathroom, set my cup down on the counter and leaned forward to look at myself in the mirror. What a sight. My hair was a mess and the deep, dark circles under my eyes showed how little sleep I was getting. Surely a nice, hot shower would help. At least I'd feel better. Maybe even help the fog lift from my brain.

I needed a clear head today and I know sleep would be a good cure for the way I was feeling. But that wasn't going to happen too soon. Sleep was hard when memories made their way into my dreams.

I turned around to reach inside the shower and turned on the water. Mandy was already in her spot in front of the open bathroom door. First the hot, then the cold, making sure the temp was right to get in. I took off my robe and gown and stepped in, letting my head soak underneath the running water. It felt good. I started crying. That was something else I was doing a lot of as of late.

Chapter 8

My mind wandered back in time again. The bed, Tami... That wonderful night when...

I was walking down a corridor of the hospital, sipping my soda as I went. I rounded a corner to see Nat and Kyle playing Uno at one of the small end tables where they sat. Don and Camille were sitting close by Kyle, watching the game. Brian was sitting on the other side watching over Nat's shoulder. He looked up as I came into the room.

I sat down in the chair closest to the hall looking toward the double doors just ahead. Waiting for someone, anyone to come out to let us know how things were going. I sat my cup down on the table next to me and picked up a magazine that was laying there.

Out of the corner of my eye I saw Brian get up walked over to where I was sitting. He sat down in the chair beside me. I didn't say anything. "It's been a long time. How you been doing?" he asked.

"I'm just great." I said not looking up from the magazine. Brian re-adjusted himself in his chair, fidgeting, as I call it. "I remember," he started to say, "the night Jeremy was born. That was some long night." He looked over at me waiting for a response.

"I remember too. I was there." I said still not looking up from the magazine. There was no way of getting out of having this conversation.

"Yeah, I know, but you were a whole lot calmer than I was. That machine making that noise... "

"It was a heart monitor" I interrupted finally looking up to meet Brian's eyes.

"Yeah. It didn't seem to bother you though" Brian said contritely.

"Might not have bothered you so much if you hadn't brought your flask that night" I retorted quickly.

"That's why I brought it. To help me stay calm." Now he was defending himself.

"It didn't work. You didn't stay calm. In fact, you got drunk, celebrating that night!" I said, then added under my breath, "As if you really needed an excuse." I put the magazine that I wasn't reading back down on the table.

I got up and walked toward the double doors. I really didn't want the night spoiled with memories that were both beautiful and disappointing.

Next thing I knew, Brian had grabbed my hand. I turned around jerking my arm away as if something was crawling up my arm. I met Brian's eyes with a definite displeasing look. I still had a hard time when it came to Brian. I didn't want to lose my temper with him reliving the past. I suppose he thought that we were past everything and we could have something special tonight while we were waiting.

I brushed past Brian to head back to the waiting room and my chair when the doors opened behind me. I looked back to see Jeremy's cheshire grin. His eyes were brilliant with his beaming smile.

"It's a girl!" he yelled so loud I thought the entire floor heard him. He raised one arm into the air, then the other while doing something like the twist. His very own little victory dance, I suppose. He grabbed me and spun me around singing "We have a girl. A beautiful baby girl."

"We have a girl!" he yelled again as the rest of the family gathered around us. Jeremy put me down then grabbed Camille and spun her around singing "We have a girl." As he put Camille back down on the floor he said proudly, "We decided on Tami Renee" he said out of breath., Camille started to tear up when she heard Jeremy. I could tell she was overjoyed they decided to name their first born daughter after Camille's grandmother.

There was so much excitement and carrying-on that it didn't take long for a nurse to come out of the double doors to ask that we quiet down a bit. Apparently we could be heard all the way back to the nurse's station. But, at least, we all got to go see Tess and Tami Renee at the same time. We just had to get dressed up for the occasion. Everyone had to get into the gowns and booties.

Tess looked so tired when we entered the room. She was sitting up in bed holding a little bundle that was wrapped in a blanket close to her chest. She quickly glanced up at the commotion then back down, a beaming smile on her face as she gazed at the bundle. Camille and Don went over to her side, each bending to kiss her forehead.

Tess looked up and asked, "Do you want to meet your granddaughter?"

"Well, of course," Camille said smiling as she put out her arms to take the baby. Don was looking over her shoulder gazing wondrously at his tiny granddaughter.

I made my way to the other side of Tess's bed and leaned to give her a kiss. "How are you feeling?"

"Great" she said beaming, "although I am a little tired."

"Well," I stated matter of factly, "we won't stay long. We'll let you get your rest. But not before I get to hold my beautiful granddaughter." I added as I started around the bed.

Camille handed me Tami Renee. I hugged and kissed my baby girl. Gazing at this beautiful bundle of joy I turned to the others in the room. Kyle and Nat were standing at the foot of the bed. As soon as they had their peak at her I turned to Brian standing behind them.

"Do you want to hold her granddaughter" I asked him.

He just smiled as he took her from me.

Chapter 9

With my eyes closed I lifted my head and let the hot water run down my face. I could feel it from the top of my head all the way down to the tip of my toes. I took a deep breath before reaching to turn the water off. I grabbed a towel off the rack and got out of the shower to dry.

Someone knocked at the bedroom door and yelled "Five minutes." Mandy started barking at the sound. They must have waken her. Then silence. I think it sounded like Colin but wasn't quite sure. Hurrying, I got dressed and headed out the bedroom door to see my three sons sitting at the table. It was Colin.

Mandy had already passed me up and was in front of Colin begging for attention. Obviously she was happy to see him. As soon as Colin saw me he got up and walked right into my arms, holding me tightly.

It was uncanny, he looked exactly like his dad. He had his stocky build with the thinning hair. That's why he kept it shaved he told me once. There just wasn't enough there to show off. He had his dad's blue eyes, too.

I wander sometimes if we had more kids what would they be like today. What would my life be like today. I definitely wouldn't have the same kids if we had stayed married.

After a moment he pulled back, slipping his arm around my waist walking me to the table. "No arguments" he said sternly wagging his finger in my face. He pulled out a chair and putting both hands on my shoulders to sit me down he then proceeded to hand me a piece of toast. *"Eat,"* Colin commanded.

I looked up at him to protest, I wasn't hungry, "Don't even think about it mom" came out of his mouth before I could say a word. "You know you need to eat something. And, look at the feast Kyle and Nat made," extending his hand at the stack of cinnamon toast sitting in the middle of the table.

"How can you refuse?" Sarcasm was heavy in his voice, but serious too. "You don't want to hurt their feelings do you? Not after all their hard work?" Now he was making fun of his brothers. All three had a plate of scrambled eggs in front of them. This was hardly a feast. But toast would do.

"Well... As long as I'm not eating alone... " I said looking around the table. "Get me some more coffee, please." I asked resigned to the fact that they looked like they would actually try to force feed me if I didn't at least get some of it down. I knew I needed to eat. I really didn't remember the last meal I had.

Of course, Mandy thought she should get some to and started to tell us about it. "No Mandy. You had your breakfast" I told her. I had to talk to her like she was still a pup at times. I guess she was at heart. So far, she didn't show any signs of age slowing her down, especially at the dinner table. When I sat down to eat, she always sat at my feet waiting to see if any scraps would fall to the floor.

With that said Kyle went to fill my coffee cup while Colin and Nat sat down at the table for their own breakfast.

"Cheri sends her love" Colin said. I smiled with a mouthful of food. "We didn't want the kids to miss any school." Colin answered the question before it was even asked. I knew that's the way it would be though. They didn't live that close, it was a fifteen hour plus drive from their home. And Colin drove it after a full day of work. He must really be tired.

Kyle set my cup in front of me then sat down. We held each other hands. Eyes closed and heads bowed, Nat began to pray, "Oh Heavenly Father, Lord of our lives, we thank you for this food set before us that will sustain our bodies. We ask you, especially today, that you hold us in your grip. To keep us and guide us through our day. Hold us tight within your grasp that we do not dishonor you. Guard us against any temptations. We love you. In the sweet, precious name of Jesus. Amen."

We all repeated 'Amen', even Colin. He grew up with his dad and was not subjected to my 'church antics', as his father would say. But he loved us and respected our faith. I quietly wandered if things might change someday, maybe today. We'd talk once in a while about God and his saving grace, yet he still wasn't ready to accept it in his heart.

"So, how was the road?" Nat asked as he put a fork full of eggs in his mouth.

"Not too bad, considering." Colin said as he took a sip of coffee then began eating. Through bites food he continued to talk. "I hit a little rush hour traffic leaving town. Other than that it was uneventful."

I took a bite of toast, chewing it slowly, when Colin told me, "The kids were upset about not being able to come. Especially Marissa. You know how she loves of Gamma" he said smiling. "She thought you needed to be taken care of. I told her that's what me and Kyle and Nat were going to do. But, she insisted that no one could take care of you like she could. She really put up a fuss" he said chuckling. "You know she's quite serious about taking care of you" as his voice turned serious like his daughter.

"That's so sweet. I'll have to call her to thank her." I paused to take another bite of toast and a sip of coffee. "Maybe she can come down this summer and spend some time with me. Just me and her. You and Cheri talk about it when you go home."

"Yes, ma'am" then finished his coffee before adding, "Maybe we ought to wait till time is closer before we say anything to Marissa." Hint, hint his eyes said to me with a wink. "She's got an elephant's memory. You know, only what she wants to remember."

"Well, of course, she does." I said as I got up to take my plate to the sink. "All kids do, especially when it's something they want. And if she wants to take care of me she can for a while this summer, after school ends. That's why you need to talk to Cheri soon so we can make tentative plans for it."

"You know how Cheri is, though. That's not going to be an easy request to fill." He sounded as if he had his doubts anything like that could happen.

"I know. We'll just have to find a way to convince her,." I said, knowing too that would take some doing.

Kyle grabbed everyone else's plates and brought them into the kitchen while we were talking.

"Maybe for about a week, I'll come get her and bring her home again. And tell Cheri I'll have Marissa call mom every single night she's away from home" I stressed.

I could see where Cheri was coming from. Marissa was their only girl and the baby to boot. Momma just didn't want to let go of her yet, she was only five.

I looked into Colin's bloodshot eyes, "Colin, you look like you need a nap" I said concerned for his health. He was getting over the flu he had just last week.

"Nah, I'm fine momma" he said not quite convincingly. His eyes were very droopy.

"Right. Of course you are. You've only been up over twenty-four hours, had a full day at work yesterday, and then, drove all last night to get here this morning." I said with a bit of heavy sarcasm myself. I knew how tired he was, he just didn't want to leave me yet. "Just for an hour or so, rest. OK?"

He looked at me with concerned eyes. It had been so long since we had seen each other and now for this. I knew he really didn't want to leave my side. He wanted to be there for me as much as his brothers did. And, yet, even with food and coffee he was having a hard time trying to keep his eyes opened while we talked.

"We'll talk later, honey" I said touching his cheek. "You get some rest. We got time." I paused. "Besides, momma knows best." I told him as I helped him up from the table and headed him toward what was now one of the guest bedrooms. He reluctantly picked up his bag on the way.

I watched as Colin closed the door before turning to go back to the kitchen. Kyle came out and stood in the doorway right in front of me. He said, "Dishes are done and the kitchen is clean. There's nothing for you to do in there." He stood there in front of me with his hands on his hips telling me he was not going to let me pass.

"Thank you." I said politely, kissed him on the cheek and turned to the living room. Mandy was close behind on my heels again.

"Is there anything else we need to do before we get ready to go?" Nat asked.

"No. I cleaned yesterday. So it's just whatever we do this morning that has to be done." I sat down in my recliner, leaned it back, and relaxed. "And that's been done." Mandy stretched out beside the chair.

"What about the pictures?" Nat asked. I had told him not to let me forget to take the picture albums.

"There." I pointed to the coffee table. There lay two photo albums that I had put together throughout the years. One consisted mainly of Jeremy growing up in this house. Yearly school pictures, sports, and an assortment of vacation pictures. The album lying underneath had pictures of his family, Tess, Tami, Ryan, Clay.

Nat and Kyle walked to the sofa and sat down, each picking up one of the albums. "Have you decided which ones you want?" Nat asked.

"I'm gonna take them both and just leave them out. Tess can do what she wants. She has a good portrait of him and the family they took last Christmas" I said quietly.

Nat opened the album he'd picked up. It was the one with our family's photos. He slowly started looking at each and every photo with Kyle looking on beside him. They commented on his baby picture saying how funny he looked with that expression.

"Watch it." I said, "All of you look almost exactly the same. Except for the hair... And the eyes."

"You're kidding." Kyle said laughing.

"You don't believe me. Go get that album over there." I pointed to the bookshelf where the other picture albums were, two each. Of course, they had to pull out their particular ones and look just to make sure. "That one there has all four of your baby pictures in it, side by side." I pointed to the brown leather album with a family tree embossed on the cover.

Kyle grabbed it to check it out. It was true. The first page held each one of their first baby pictures with all their particulars written under each one. Actually, they were the pictures the hospitals had taken when they were born. Eyes wide, they started laughing at the comparison. "Colin's got to see this" Nat said as he stood up to head for the bedroom.

"You can wait till he gets up." I said hearing him get to his feet. I might have my eyes closed but I still knew when the boys were up to mischief.

"Well, of course." He said as he suddenly changed directions. "Did you really think I was going to go bursting in there just to show him how dorky he looked?" he asked trying to sound offended.

He was now headed to the kitchen instead of the hall. "I'm getting something to drink."

"I wouldn't put it past you" I told him as he passed by me.

Again, they both laughed.

Chapter 10

I sat back again closing my eyes and thought about when I put that last picture in that album. Nathaniel was the orneriest of all four of my boys, even before he was born. He definitely wasn't like his brothers in that respect. It was pretty much tough luck if I didn't like it.

Nat was more comfortable lying sideways in my belly than any other position. And as he got bigger, he got to be more and more of a pain. It wasn't comfortable having a foot stick out of my side while I was trying to sleep because he decided to stretch.

And, if that wasn't enough, he had to be difficult coming out, too. I think if he could have come out sideways he would have. But the doctors didn't agree with that idea.

"Are you sure?" the doctor asked as she was examining me.

"Yes" I said through the discomfort she was inflicting on me. She was not being gentle trying to see how far I was dilated. I suppose she thought it might be like before, false labor.

"Well... I think we need to do a sonogram to see how this baby is laying then." She abruptly turned to the nurse and asked her to bring the machine over.

They hooked it up and turned it on. The doctor bared my big belly, put the goop on the sonogram and began to rub it on me.

"Ohhh... That's cold" I said shivering from the cold gel.

The doctor didn't say anything. She kept an eye on the machine to find the baby laying breech. She pointed out the feet on one side and the head on the other.

"It's very risky to try to have this baby like this. What I'd like to do is give you a shot to stop the contractions then turn the baby the right way." She was very serious as she spoke. There was real concern about this situation she didn't want to get further complicated.

"All right" I managed to say right before another contraction hit.

Brian was sitting in the chair beside my bed watching television. He looked over when the doctor started talking to me about the danger of a breech birth. It wasn't until then that he got up and came over to the bed beside me.

We just looked at each, waiting while the nurse and doctor left to prepare for the procedure. It wasn't long before the nurse came back to give me the shot. It took about half an hour to take effect.

The nursing staff moved me to a gurney to take me to another room. They let Brian tag along.

With one doctor on one side and the other doctor on the other side, they pushed him into position. It worked with one exception. After another examination they discovered that the baby's cord had fallen too.

I was able to get a little sleep while the shot they gave me was still affective. It didn't seem long, though, before the contractions started up again. This was going to be a very long night.

The doctor had me hooked up to all sort of monitors, for me and the baby. By morning the monitor showed that the baby was in distress. That's when the doctors decided it was time to do a C-section.

Of course, by that time, Brian was drunk as a skunk. He insisted that we go home to have the baby. He insisted that I call his mom to have her talk me out of the c-section. I know he was too drunk, but I think he was also too scared of the surgery.

He finally relented after explaining several times that my life and the life of the baby were in danger. At least, he still got to attend the birth. He was excited about that.

Although, the doctors did have to tell him more than once to move his head back over the curtain. Brian was standing behind me to watch.

Well, Nat ended up being a C-section baby. Like I said, Nat was ornery and one big pain right from the very beginning.

We were in the hospital for a week. Brian was home taking care of Jeremy and Kyle with his mom's help. Surprisingly, the house was pretty cleaned the day Nathaniel and I came home.

Jeremy and Kyle were so excited having a baby brother. They kept trying to help me with him, asking to hold him. Kyle even offered to change his diaper once until he found out how bad it smelled. Then he just called him 'stinky'.

Chapter 11

My mind came back to the present when I heard the boys laughing again. I listened intently when they started recounting the events that lead to that one series of pictures they were looking at.

It was on one of our weekend camping trips in the mountains. We set up camp near the waterfalls where we were going fishing. The boys help set up the tent and then gathered wood for the fire before getting out the fishing gear. Brian showed them how to get the line ready. Then he gave instructions on casting the line.

He did this every fishing trip we had been on since we started a couple of years ago. Besides, the boys weren't old enough they needed constant reminders.

I was taking pictures of Brian and the boys as they were casting their lines It was funny watching them throw their lines in the water. Brian flicked his pole back behind him then forward to the water. The boys were watching when he slipped. I pressed the button on the camera just as he fell in the water. We all broke out laughing.

I got it. He got up and shook himself off then cast again, this time without falling in. It was a beautiful picture of father and sons silhouetted in the noon sun against the mountains. Another perfect picture. I captured some great pictures of them standing at the water's edge.

The picture Kyle and Nat were laughing about was the one where Brian had caught a pretty big fish. He had to get a picture because he thought it was a record breaker. Just as I snapped the shot, the fish started to wiggle, slapping Brian in the stomach. It was another perfect picture.

I heard the door open down the hall. Footsteps. I opened my eyes to see Colin coming into the room. "I thought you were going to try to get some rest?"

"I did rest." He said. "Couldn't sleep though, too much noise out here. You know how loud you guys are? Sounds like a pack of hyenas" Colin managed to say between yawns. Although, they really did sound that way.

He walked over to the couch and sat down by Nat to see what they were laughing at. Colin listened intently as Nat described in detail the events of the picture. Then they all started laughing again. Memories.

Nat started flipping the pages regaling us all with stories about each of the pictures. Of course, Kyle had to add his own version. I think they seem to forget that Colin was in most of them too. Even though he lived with his dad, he was not excluded from our weekend trips. He went with us most of the time.

Of course, Colin had his own version. Listening quietly, it amazed me of how similar, yet so different, the recounting could be. But the memories were good.

They quieted down when the cam across a picture of Jeremy standing proudly with the catch of the day. His was pole on one side and the fish on the other. He was holding the fishing line with the fish dangling from the hook. It was only about three inches long. He was so proud because he caught it all by himself.

I sat there with my eyes closed listening to the boys recounting their own version of stories from their childhood when the phone rang. They stopped talking as soon as I reached for my phone.

"Hello." They were watching me intently.

"How are you doing, sweetie?" I asked, concern now in my voice.

"No, honey, that won't be any problem. We have it right here."

"All right, we'll see you in a little bit then."

"I love you too. Bye."

I put the phone back down on the table beside me then looked up to see the boys still watching me, waiting. They seem to know who I had been talking to.

"Tess wants us to bring a certain picture." I said as I sat up to grab one of the albums. The one with Jeremy sitting behind Tess on the hospital bed holding their beloved daughter. She had said so many times that she was going to steal that picture because it showed who Jeremy really was. A loving husband. A proud and devoted father.

"This one." I removed it from its jacket and got up. "I guess it's time to change. They're about ready to leave."

Mandy had jumped up when I started moving. I looked at her, "You ready to go outside girl? We have to go bye-bye in a little bit." She was a very smart dog. She knew there was something going on with all the boys here today. She could sense it more now.

I walked to the back door and opened it, Mandy went rushing out. I shut the door and headed down the hall to my room. I had already put out what I was going to wear. So that was a no brainer.

Nat called out before I reached my door. "Mom, I'm going to go get Candy. We'll see you there."

I had stopped and turned to see Nat coming down the hall while we were talking. "Ok, hon. Drive carefully" I said. We kissed on the cheeks to say good-bye. I turned and walked into my bedroom shutting the door behind me.

Time seemed to be moving fast today. At least right now it was. I hoped the whole day could be like this. 'Please, God,' I prayed, not wanting this day to drag out any longer than it had to. 'Just help me through the next couple of hours.'

Time, I thought, *really did move fast in a lifetime.* I remembered the day each of my sons were born. I remembered their first steps. The first time they fed themselves without any help. What a mess. I even remembered the first time each of them got their very first scar. Each one had such a traumatic event.

Colin was running behind the bleachers at the ball park when he fell on a piece of glass causing a deep gash across his palm. He was seven.

Jeremy was nine when he had appendicitis. He was the extremist. He just had to outdo his brothers.

Kyle was four when he sliced his finger trying to open a bag of candy.

Nat fell at the base of the park bench spitting open his upper lip all the way to the tip of his nose. Now, that's a Fourth of July picnic none of us will ever forget.

Chapter 12

It was a bright, sunny afternoon at the park. Perfect mid-day weather for a cookout. There were lots of people out here enjoying this beautiful God given day. Brian's family and mine got together. Family gatherings were big when we did.

I was standing with my hand covering my eyes, straining to find the kids in the bright sunshine. They'd all taken off for the playground for some fun while the adults were getting everything set up and ready to cook. Everybody liked days like this, especially me. I didn't have to do quite as much; at least I didn't have to cook. That was Brian's job today.

I saw Nat on the monkey bars, he just loved climbing up and down and all around. He was pretty flexible and very resilient. That's what made him so fast.

"Colin," I yelled, "he's over there" pointing toward Nat. Colin was a pretty good babysitter looking after his younger brothers when we came here. Kyle was at the swings and Jeremy was playing tetherball.

Colin looked over to where I was pointing then raised his arm in acknowledgment. He started jogging over to his youngest brother.

Satisfied, I turned back around to unpack some of the things we'd brought. The usual, paper plates, plastic cups, soda.... Everything you need for a beautiful fun day at the park.

Brian was at the grill trying to get it started. His philosophy, the more coal, the better. It didn't matter to him that he wasted at least half of it with this technique. But still, he was the one cooking. So I didn't say anything about it.

I looked up when I heard Nat screaming. I saw Colin had him in a head lock, wrestling him to the ground. Nat let out another squeal before Colin freed him, laughing. Nat reached out and swung at his mean older brother. He actually connected then tore off running in the opposite direction.

Nat looked back to see if Colin was following him. Of course he was. He wasn't going to let his little brother get away with punching him in the jaw.

I guess he'll think twice next time he does that I thought. Don't want to get to close to someone you get mad.

I watched Colin running after Nat when he yelled "Stop!" Nat was looking back at Colin chase him and didn't have time to turn his head forward before he stumbled and fell flat on his face. The momentum of his run propelled him straight into one of the park benches.

Colin was there in a split second to pick up his brother when he called for me. Nat was screaming and crying. He'd been hurt. I dropped whatever I had in my hands and started running toward them. My heart was pounding.

When I got there, I fell to my knees to see what had happened. We quickly got a crowd of kids around us to see what they could see. There was blood all over Nat's face and on his shirt. It was a bloody mess. Nat had landed on the cement base that held the bench in place.

I had to literally pull Nat's hands away from this face. Blood was coming through his fingers. "Nat! Let me see!" I demanded. There was blood all over his mouth and nose. You could plainly see the gash that extended from the tip on his nose to his upper lip. I scooped him up into my arms and headed for the tent to get my keys. Brian was coming toward us.

"What happened?" he demanded to know.

"He's hurt. What do you think" I said curtly. "I'm taking him to the hospital."

"Let me see." Brian demanded as he grabbed my arm. We stopped just long enough for him to check out the injury. "Ah, it's not that bad" he said with a little smirk.

"He'll be Ok" he added as he tousled Nat's hair. Nat just started crying harder.

"No he won't, Brian!" I yelled. "That's a deep gash and I want a doctor to look at it. He'll probably need stitches." Nat let out a scream when he heard me say that.

I hated it when Brian was drinking. It irritated me beyond belief because nothing seemed too important to matter to him. This wasn't the time to make light of the situation.

I pushed past him in a hurry to get to the car. Then the thought struck that maybe Brian was trying to calm Nat in his own way.

"Mom, I'm sorry," Colin was yelling to be heard over Nat. He was running behind me. "I tried to stop him! Honest!" The worry and concern in his voice was overwhelming. It showed me how upset he was about the whole thing. He sounded close to tears himself.

"I know you did, Colin. I was watching" I said huffing and puffing the words as we moved quickly up the slope.

"I'm sorry Nat. I really am." Colin was trying to tell his brother. Begging for forgiveness.

Nat didn't answer. He was too busy crying in my arms. His little hands holding the towel to his nose that we picked up when we got the car keys,.

When we finally got to the car Colin helped me put Nat in his car seat then got in beside him. "Colin, you need to stay with your brothers."

"Mom... Nat needs me right now." Colin said desperately.

Maybe it would be better for the ride to the hospital. He could help keep Nat calmer and not go into an explosive episode that I couldn't do anything about it. That wouldn't help me drive.

I looked back to see Grams coming to the car, Jeremy and Kyle running up with her. She asked how bad and I told her as quick as I could. Then I asked her to watch the other two. "Of course. You just be careful." She said giving me a quick hug. Her voice was full with concern.

"Mom, we want to come" Jeremy and Kyle insisted.

"Sorry boys. Not this time. You won't be able to do anything anyway. You'd just get bored sitting around the hospital."

"But squirt needs us" they protested.

"Not this time I said!" I said sternly enough their eyes dropped to the ground.

Nat looked at Jeremy, then to Colin sitting beside him, then back to Jeremy.

"Don't worry Nat," Jeremy was saying, "we'll get him back, right?" He said looking at Kyle.

"But I tried to stop him" Colin was saying. Too bad his brothers weren't listening.

"You're gonna get it, just wait and see." Kyle had to put in. He sounded like he really meant it too. Colin just sighed shaking his head then turned his attention back to his little brother.

Chapter 13

It took fifteen very long minutes to get into the emergency room of the hospital. The nurses took one look at Nat's injury before she got up from behind her station to hurry us back into one of the rooms. She let Colin come with us.

The doctor came in as soon as we got to the room. I tried to sit Nathaniel down on the exam table. He wasn't having any of it. He started kicking and screaming again. So I had to sit down with him on my lap.

Poor doctor, Nat wouldn't let him even look at his nose. He lay there in my arms with his hands over his nose, shaking his head back and forth. Which only made the pain worse and Nat cry more. I had to literally pry Nat's hands from his face and hold them at his side. That didn't work very well either.

We tried coaxing him to be still so the doctor could take a good look. All our efforts were to no avail. So the doctor told me he wanted to sedate Nat so he properly exam the wound without the flailing arms of a hysterical child.

I agreed. He left and a nurse came in a short time later to give Nat the shot. That was still easier said than done. But we managed.

After a few minutes Nat started settling down and getting drowsy. Colin had come over from the chair he had been sitting in to talk to Nat. "The doctor just wants to see so he can fix you all up. He just wants to make you all better." His eyes trying to encourage Nat.

I let Nat fall asleep in my arms before laying him on the exam table. The nurse put on a papoose wrap on him. This was going to help when the doctor came back in, which wasn't long. I thanked God silently.

He cleaned the wound and did a bit of pulling this way and that, looking closely. He finally decided that it really did need a few stitches. I gave my permission, more papers to sign.

But before the doctor could do anything else another nurse came in asking for him. He excused himself and left the room. Now all Colin and I could do was sit and wait for the doctor to return.

We talked a bit about what happened to get us here this Fourth of July. I could tell how badly Colin felt just by the way he spoke. He was so upset that he was the one that caused the accident.

"Accidents happen Colin" I said trying to sooth his hurt. "And I don't see how you could have foreseen this happening when you started chasing Nat. Do you?" I had to try to get him to let go of some of the guilt he obviously felt.

"No" he said softly.

"Then quit feeling like you could have stopped something you had no control over" I stressed.

"Yes ma'am" he was sitting back in his chair staring at Nat sleeping on the table. "He just looks scary all wrapped up like a mummy."

"I know" I said trying to console him. "But he's going to be all right" I paused slightly. "We just have to wait for the doctor to come back."

We had to wait nearly two hours before the doctor did come back. We found out later that there had been a bad accident and several other people were coming in to the ER. His services were needed elsewhere.

When the doctor did return, the nurse didn't come with him. So he asked me play nurse and assist him by putting my arms over Nat in case he started to wake during the procedure.

I did as the doctor asked and looked over to Colin. He sat in a chair opposite me watching the doctor. His eyes widened when the doctor started stitching then closed them tight. Thank God Nat didn't wake. He just lay there quietly, peacefully.

When the doctor finished he told me the nurse would be in shortly to give Nat another shot to wake him up. They wanted to flush the drugs from his system. We would have to wait a while before we could go.

The nurse came and went quickly. But not before she took off the papoose to give Nat the shot. I sat back down next to Nat on the table. I was so exhausted I laid my head down on the table.

Colin came back into the room when he saw the doctor leave. He had slipped out when the doctor started stitching up Nat's nose. I don't blame him. If I could have, I think I would have done the same thing.

We were sitting there quietly when all of the sudden Nat sat straight up on the table then slumped back down. His eyes never opened. Colin and I jumped out of our seats when he did that. It scared both of us to bits.

We looked at each other then back at Nat on the table. He didn't move again. I bolted for the door to find a nurse in the hall and told her what had just happened. She said 'not to worry, that was the drugs flushing out of his system. We could probably leave in about an hour.

Chapter 14

It was dark when we finally left the hospital. Nat was sound asleep as I carried him to the car in my arms. Colin carried my purse and keys for me. He unlocked and open the back door for me to put Nat in his seat. Then he got in beside his brother again putting his arm around him after he buckled in himself.

We rode home in silence. I looked back once to see Colin's head on his chest. He had fallen asleep too.

"Colin. We're home" I said softly. He stirred a little before stretching out his arms. Then he opened one eye and then the other.

The house was dark when we got there. I suppose everyone was still at the park watching the fireworks. Nat's going to be so disappointed he missed them. "We'll do something tomorrow." I whispered to my sleeping son. Right now all I wanted to do was get him in bed for the night.

Once inside I carried Nat to his bed, took off his shoes and tucked him in. Colin crawled in next to his baby brother and put his arm around him protecting him from further harm. He kissed his brother on the check and laid his head down on the pillow next to Nat. In a split second, they were both asleep.

I went to take a quick shower to wash the events of the day off. I put on my gown and robe then went to the living room to wait for the others to get home.

I had just sat down on the sofa when the rest of my crew came in. Grams and Gramps drove them home. *Thank the Lord for Brian's parents* I thought. What a blessing. They came in to ask about Nat before leaving. I explained what had happened and that we just got home about half an hour before them.

Jeremy and Kyle wanted to go see Nat, but I wouldn't let them. I told them they could see him tomorrow after a good night sleep.

Instead, they started to regale me with stories about the fireworks we missed. Colin had gotten up to sit beside me when the crowd came in. He was such a light sleeper. It didn't take much to wake him, especially when it came to his brothers.

We started listening to Jeremy and Kyle's stories when Grams interrupted to say 'Good night.' They were too tired to go through the telling.

"Good night. And thanks for everything." I said as I kissed them good-bye.

The boys were definitely too wired to go to bed yet. We sat and listened to all the fancy descriptions of just about each and every firework, of course. Brian had to add his version too. But I really didn't care what Brian had to say right now. He was drunk enough and had a beer in his hand when they came in. I'm glad his parents were there to take care of the boys.

Brian and I argued again last night after all the kids went to sleep. I went to bed angry because Brian was drunk. He couldn't take care of his kids when he was that way. His parents had to.

I woke later, restless, to find him passed out on the couch. I had gotten up to find lights and the TV still on. I shut them off and slipped in to check on Nat. He was still sleeping soundly when I lay down next to him.

The next morning I woke up in Nat's bed. I opened my eyes to the light coming into the room thru the curtained windows. I started to get out of bed when Nat suddenly threw his arms around my neck and pulled me back down on the pillow. I looked at him. His eyes were barely open, just a slither. "Momma," he said, barely audible, "my head hurts."

"I know honey." I said as soothingly as I could. I brought my hand up to gently rub his forehead. Then let it rest on his shoulder. "You ready to get up? Get something in that belly?" We hadn't eaten since breakfast yesterday. "What would you like?"

He looked at me for a minute. He was thinking. His eyes betraying thoughts of what he could get away with.

"Ice cream?!" he queried.

"I don't think so. Think of something else, maybe pancakes?" I quickly asked seeing the disappointed look on his face. There's that puppy dog look.

He closed one eye to think hard if he wanted pancakes. "With chocolate syrup?" he asked.

"Really?" I shouldn't be surprised. "Well, I suppose you could this one time." I stressed.

"But only me" he stated, determined he should be the only one to get special treatment.

"Pancakes? No. Pancakes are for everyone." He gave me his displeased look until I said, "The chocolate syrup is all yours today though. The others will have to make do with just regular syrup."

He smiled then winced in pain. He let me go so I could make him his special breakfast. We'll see if this was a good idea.

In the kitchen I was cooking more pancakes while Nat was sitting at the table with his special chocolate pancakes when we heard some strange noises coming down the hall. Suddenly Colin came struggling in from the hall with Jeremy hanging on his back, his arms wrapped around

Colin's neck. Kyle was attached to Colin's leg being dragged behind him.

"Help me. Help me, Nat!" Colin was saying. "They won't let go!"

Nat sat there giggling, "OW". His eyes were big and bright, smiling at the funny sight.

Jeremy and Kyle wouldn't let go until Colin fell at Nat's feet..

"I told you we'd get him!" Jeremy exclaimed. "Now it's your turn."

Nat reached down and slapped Colin on the forehead.

Colin rolled over with Jeremy and Kyle still hanging on. He trapped them underneath him as he did. Then proceeded to tickle his captives.

Chapter 15

I put my shoes on, grabbed my purse and headed out the bedroom door.

Kyle and Colin were waiting for me in the living room. Someone already let Mandy in. She was sitting between them on the couch when I entered. When she saw me, she immediately got down from the couch to come to me, wagging her tail for affection.

I bent down to scratch her head, "Watch the house for me girl. We gotta go. We'll be back later." I turned toward the door, the boys not far behind.

"One of you got the picture albums?" I asked as we were walking to the car.

"I got it." Colin replied as we got into the car. Kyle was our driver today. He wouldn't let me or Colin drive because of the amount of sleep we'd had, or should I say, didn't have.

The drive was deafeningly quiet. I thought we were most likely solemn because of what the rest of this day held in store for us. Right now, this was the easy part. When we got there I would have to talk to Brian.

A few cars where already there when we arrived. It was nice to be so close to the front, third in line. We didn't have to walk far to the doors. As I got out of the car I realized just how stiff I was again from the long ride. So I walked slowly until I could move more freely again.

As we entered the building I saw Tess putting some things on a table. I held out my hand to Colin and he gave the photo we brought. Holding the picture tightly, I took a deep breath and straightened my posture. I was trying to fight back the tears forming in my eyes yet again.

I slowly walked over to Tess and touched her on the shoulder. When she didn't look up from the pictures she just put down I waited silently. I waited for her to look at me or to say something to tell me she knew I was there.

When she did I handed her the picture she had asked me for earlier. She looked at it a moment then laid it beside another one on the table. A tear rolled down her cheek.

I couldn't help it, the emotions were too overwhelming. I put both my arms around her shoulders, laying my head aside hers. We both started crying. Tess turned to fully embrace me in a hug. I don't know how long we stood there just trying to comfort each other. The only sound from either of us were our sobs.

Suddenly, I felt an arm grab my waist. I opened my eyes long enough to see Tami had joined us. She had come over to wrap her arms around her mom and grandma. A loving gesture from a loving girl. I moved my arm from Tess to Tami so I could hold her too. Tightly embracing both my girls. Tess had been my daughter for nearly eighteen years now, long before it became official.

Tess pulled back a little when Tami came over. Now she turned to put both her arms around her ten year old daughter, giving her a big hug. Tami looked so much like her father. Especially with her golden brown hair and brown eye. His eyes.

Tess looked up at me and said, "Brian's here. I think he went outside for a smoke. But he's looking for you" she said in a low voice. I could see the sadness in her eyes as she spoke.

"God," I prayed, "help us all through this day, especially now." I didn't know what to expect out of Brian. He could be his predictable self or actually, hopefully, a decent man today. I really hadn't seen or talked to him much in years, but the boys said he had changed a lot. *We'll see* I thought skeptically, hopefully.

I decided not to go looking for him, he'd find me soon enough. Instead I looked around at how everything had been arranged. On this table, Tess had place an arrangement of pictures that told the story of their life together. A high school dance, college graduation, her marriage to Jeremy, their one mission trip to Thailand after a hurricane had devastated it and more of his family life.

Beside the table was a beautiful arrangement of Arudina, commonly known as bamboo orchids. They both fell in love with the orchid on their trip to Thailand. They we told that it represented love, beauty, strength and virility. That's what they wanted their marriage to be, full of life. And it was.

They made sure each and every day was filled with the joy of God's love bursting at the seams. They were so happy together, devoted to one another as well as family and friends. God had truly blessed them so very much with all that life could possibly hold.

My gazed turned toward the coffin. It was silver in color with another arrangement lying on top. This was a closed casket funeral. There had been so much... I couldn't bring myself to say it much less think it.

Nat and Candy came up behind me. They obviously saw the tears rolling down my cheek and with their arms of embrace they scurried me away to the side room. Brian came in with us followed closely by Colin and Kyle, who shut the door behind him. If there was going to be a scene, he didn't want anyone else to see it.

Brian abruptly pushed Nat to the side and put his arms around me, trying to hold me. I instinctively pushed him away with force. I had no desire to have him touch me.

"What, in God's name, do you think you're doing?!" It was almost a yell, but not quite. I was definitely appalled and cross with his actions.

"Baby, I just wanted to... " he started when I cut him off.

"Don't 'Baby' me. You don't have any right what-so-ever to 'Baby' me." I said as I backed away from his grip. "In fact, you don't have any rights, any more with me."

He looked hurt and dumb-founded when I said that. I think it was more confusion than anything.

"Brian, you gave up all those rights a long, long time ago." I spoke crossly to him, appalled that he would even think he had the right to try to comfort me. It made my stomach churn.

"I just wanted... " he started to say.

Again I interrupted, "I know what you wanted. But you can't have what you want. You threw us away a long time ago when you almost killed Kyle."

He backed up a step or two. Now he really did look like I had just slapped him hard across the face. No one had said a word about that accident for years. It might have been forgiven, but it wasn't forgotten, not by me anyway. The memory of that night came rushing back with a vengeance.

Chapter 16

I ran through the automatic doors just as they were opening. The nurse's station was right in front of me. I barely stopped in time to keep from running into it. My hands slapped the countertop, "I'm Kirsten Myer. I got a call that my son Kyle was here." Anxious, worried, outraged A rampant of emotions ran throughout my body and my mind hearing that my husband and young sons had been involved in an accident.

"Just a moment, please." The nurse said calmly as she typed something into her computer.

She looked up to say, "I'll take you back" as she rose from her chair. We headed down the hall through the double doors of the emergency room. I walked closely beside her peering behind every curtain to see if I could see my family. The nurse continued walking only to stop by a closed door. I stopped beside her as she opened it. There were my three babies.

Nat was in Jeremy's lap sitting by the examination table that Kyle was laying on. Nat was crying. When he saw me he jumped out of Jeremy's arms and ran to me. I scooped him up in my arms as I entered the room. Holding him tightly as I walked over to the other boys. I had to see them. The nurse shut the door behind me saying that she would tell the doctor I was here.

I was so relieved to see that Nat and Jeremy didn't appear to be hurt. They did looked scared half to death though. I looked over at Kyle, he had not gotten up when I came into the room. His head leaned toward the right with the left side up. I let out a gasp when I saw that the left side of his face had a gash two to three inches long.

The door opened, the doctor walked in. "Mrs. Myer, I'm Dr... " I didn't catch his name, my mind was reeling. I looked up from Kyle to see, what I thought was a very young doctor,

"The good news is that is that they are all O.K. Jeremy and Nat here," he smiled at Nat, "they have a few contusions and will have some bruising. They can go home when we're done here, but keep a close eye on them for a night or two to make sure there's no concussion.

He paused a moment to turn his attention to Kyle, then added, "Kyle, here, is a little different story. As you can tell, he sustained a pretty nasty gash. We'll have to clean and stitch it up, but I think he should be able to go home too."

There was a pause as I looked at him, my mouth open. I was concentrating so hard on what he was saying it almost didn't register. I must have been holding my breath because I heard it come out of my mouth. My hand went over my heart, "Oh, thank God."

"You'll just need to sign some papers for the procedure then we can get started." He was looking at me.

"OK" I managed to say.

"Great. I'll send the nurse in with the papers."

"Thank you," I said softly.

He shut the door behind him as he left. I turned back around to look at Kyle and Jeremy. Nat was still in my arms. "What happened?" I asked. They all started talking at once. I could only make out a word here and there. "Ok, ok," I finally said. "Let's try this one at a time."

"Daddy wrecked the car!" Nat was yelling in my ear between sobs.

I looked to Jeremy, "Nat and I were asleep in the back when all the sudden we were rolling over and over, I don't know how many times. Then we just stopped."

I looked at Kyle, "Where were you Kyle?"

"In the front" was all he said in a low voice.

"Were you awake?" I asked Kyle.

"Yeah" he said softly.

"Did you see what happened?" I hated to keep pushing. It was frustrating trying to get answers when it was obvious he didn't want to talk about it. He just looked at me.

"Kyle, answer me!"

He sighed before saying "all I know is dad hit something," He was in tears. I guess the interrogation was over.

The nurse came in with a clipboard in her hand. She went over what the papers were I had to sign. I had to pry Nat from my arms so he could sit on Jeremy's lap while I signed them. While I was doing that the nurse leaned over and asked me to step outside for a minute, alone.

I turned back to the boys as she was walking out and told them I would be 'right back'. And, 'no' they didn't need to come with me.

Chapter 17

I walked out of the room and shut the door behind me. The nurse was waiting a few steps away. When the door closed she started walking a few doors down. There was a policeman standing outside the door she stopped at. "This officer would like to speak to you." She said then turned and walked away.

"Is Brian Myer your husband?" he asked curtly

"Yes. What happened?" I asked anxiously.

"Where were you last evening?" the policeman asked.

"I went to bed early with a migraine. Why?" I almost felt like I was being accused of something.

"Did you know your husband went out with the children last night?" the officer asked, sounding a bit disgusted.

"No" I was getting upset with all this questioning. "What's going on?" I demanded to know.

"Ma'am, at 2:15 a.m. I was dispatched to the scene of a traffic accident." He was watching me as he spoke. Gauging my reaction I suppose. "Upon arriving at the scene, I saw a blue Impala sitting in the middle of a corner vacant lot." He took a breath before continuing, "As I approached the vehicle I heard children screaming and crying."

'Oh, God. Brian's dead' was the first thought that went through my mind. I restrained myself from saying anything and let the officer go on. I stood there staring at him, waiting for the bad news.

"My partner and I quickly assessed any injuries might have been sustained before removing the children from the car. The EMT's had arrived shortly thereafter and took them to the ambulance to attend their injuries. I then proceeded to see about the driver."

"He was unconscious at the time." He took another breath. Was that a sound of disgust I heard? "He clearly smelled of alcohol."

I backed up a step as if I had been slapped. My eyes were open wide.

"We were able to get him out of the car without much difficulty. He apparently had a bloody nose, but was still unconscious."

I looked up at the policeman in utter surprise. What was he saying? "What happened?!" I asked slowly and sternly, making sure I stressed each and every word.

By the look on his face, he did not want to tell me any more of this story. But he took another deep breath and continued, again, "From the story I got from the eldest boy, Jeremy," he looked down at his pad checking his notes, "They were at Joe's Bar and Grill tonight. They apparently snuck out to get something to eat around 11:00 p.m. I guess the kids thought it was some kind of adventure going out in the middle of the night with dad."

"What?" my heart was pounding.

"Uh, your husband apparently doesn't remember anything about the accident" now he definitely did sound curt and didn't seem to care to hide it. "In fact," he added, "he doesn't seem to remember much of anything this evening" he paused "at all". He waited for a response.

"You mean my husband, their father," I said pointing down the hall toward the room my children were in, "was so drunk he passed out in the car while driving our children home?!" My voice was getting louder at the thought of something like this actually happening.

'Apparently' the officer's eyes said but did not voice that opinion. He continued, "We do know that he was above the legal limit. He'll be charged with DUI and reckless endangerment of minor children. There may be more by the end of the investigation."

I just glared. I was feeling so disgusted and angry and I don't know what else. I could 'spit nails' as my grandma use to say. I think that's way beyond angry. And, that's exactly how I felt.

"He's inside if you want to see him?" the officer said jerking his head toward the closed door behind him. My enraged thoughts interrupted..

"NO!" I said definitely. "You'd have to arrest me for assault if I... " I paused closing the eyes to try to gain a little composure. "You can have him" I said angrily at the events just recounted to me.

He had grinned, probably imagining me in there beating up my husband for what he had just done. I almost bet he'd let me, too. Probably even walk away to get some coffee so there would be no witnesses.

He changed his expression quickly, "You just take care of those little ones in there and let us take care of this one."

I nodded in agreement too angry to say anything then turned back toward the room my sons were in.

It was about 7:00 a.m. when we finally got home from the hospital. We were all just so tired, I didn't even feel like going to church that Sunday. I decided it would be Ok to stay home this one time. Besides, we really did have a good reason.

I called Karen, a friend, to let her know what happened and that we weren't going to be there today. She said she would let the others in out class know and put us on the prayer list. I thanked her and went to bed myself.

Brian came in late that night after being released on bail. He didn't say anything. He just packed a bag to leave. We had talked countless times about his drinking, how destructive it was for our family. He knew the talking was over. There was no use in trying now. It didn't matter if he remembered the accident or not. He knew he had done one of the worse things he could do. He got his son hurt.

The next day I went to see a lawyer to file for divorce. I wasn't going to continue living like this and put my children in danger. Not ever again.

I found out later that week Brian had plead guilty to all charges the officer told me about. He did not go before a forgiving judge. He didn't try talk his way out of this time. He was sentenced to eight years and with good behavior he'd be out in less time.

I also found out that Joe's Bar and Grill had charges brought against them. I think it was something about them letting Brian leave with the kids knowing how drunk he was.

What a year this had been.

Chapter 18

Colin stepped in-between Brian and me. He wanted to put some distance between us as fast as he could. He was being very protective and was not going to let things get any worse, not today of all days.

"That was an accident" Brian said in a hurt voice.

"You were passed out drunk." My voice had gone low with anger. Maybe I hadn't really forgiven him. God help me. Every time I dwelled on things like this my anger returns. I just can't seem to let it fully go.

Our eyes met for a moment and my heart softened before I continued, "You pushed me way beyond my limits, God forgive me. But I wasn't going to have my boys raised in a home like that. You decided, remember." My eyes were tearing again. But this time it was for what we all had lost.

Already feeling the rage dissipate, "Look, Brian. I know you changed when you got out. You made it right with the boys. But you threw us away."

Brian turned around and left the room. Kyle grabbed my shoulders, looked me in the eye then kissed my forehead before he followed after his father. He knew he was needed.

I suddenly felt someone squeezing my hand. I looked to my right where Nat was standing right beside me. He was holding my clenched fist in one hand and had his other hand gripping my arm. "Thought you might actually throw a punch or something" he said softly.

My expression changed to one of confusion. I glanced around the room. It was still only us in here. "I'm sorry." I said solemnly when I realized what I had done. "I'm so sorry," I said shaking my head. "God help my unforgiving heart. I can talk to the man, but I can't abide his touch."

"It's Ok, mom. We know." Colin turned to put his arms around me.

"It's not Ok Colin. I shouldn't react like that" I said feeling dirty. "Lord" I prayed, "Help me. Forgive my unforgiving heart when these memories dwell inside me. Forgive my sin of anger and causing pain to this man who already is in pain. He grieves for his son too." The others had gathered and put their arms around me.

I continued to pray without stopping, "Lord, wrap your loving arms of grace around me that I may be able to provide some measure of comfort to all who need it today, even Brian. Thank you Lord Jesus, Savior of my soul. May your light shine brightly today. In your sweet, precious name I pray. Amen."

Nat, Candy and Colin said 'Amen'.

I backed out of the embrace and sighed, rubbing my face with my hands. I had to get my wits about me. This wasn't the time to go losing it. I had to keep it together, just a little while longer. 'God help me' I prayed silently again.

Colin opened the door to find Don on the other side. He looked a little startled. "We're getting ready to start." He said, then went to join his wife and daughter on the pew.

I told Nat he should probably find 'your dad and Kyle to let them know. They needed to be here too.

Nat went off to look for his father and brother. Colin, Candy and I sat down on the pew behind Tess and her family. Kyle and Brian joined us at the other end of the pew.

"Brian" I whispered, "I just wanted to say that I'm sorry for my outburst in there" pointing to the room we just left." "And also," I continued, "to ask your forgiveness for the hurtful way I spoke. The tongue can be very wicked."

I looked at him as I reached across and squeezed his hand. "Of course" was all he said.

The minister went to the pulpit. He opened the ceremony with a short prayer. Then we sang a couple of hymns that were favorites of Jeremy's. As I sat there my mind wandered to that fateful night.

Chapter 19

I woke to the phone ringing on my nightstand. "This better be good." I answered curtly looking at the clock to see the time. "You know what time it is?" I said a bit cross. Everyone knew I didn't like phone calls this late at night. Unless...

"Mom," I heard. It was Tess. Her voice was shaking terribly. Something's wrong, I could hear it in her voice. "Mom, it's Tess." She's crying.

"Honey, what... what's wrong? What happened?!" I was frantic. My heart started pounding in my chest as my mind went racing across the universe at the possibilities. There was someone talking in the background. And what was that noise?

"Mom, there's been an accident. We on our way to the hospital." My heart started pounding even harder with fear. 'Oh, my Lord' I prayed.

"Jeremy's been hurt real bad," she said through her tears. "He told me I had to call you. He needed to tell you something. He said it couldn't wait, mom" Tess managed to say. Then I heard her tell Jeremy I was on the phone as she placed it next to him.

I sat dumb-founded, waiting. My heart was pounding loudly in my ears.

"Mom?" I heard him say. His voice was weak, unsteady. I could hear the labored breathing as he spoke. I also heard a beeping sound in the background. I heard a siren as well.

"I'm here, baby." I said, still gripped in fear, my voice shaking. This can't be good if he can't wait to tall me. Not even till we get to the hospital.

"I.. just.. wanted to.. say.. 'I love you" Jeremy's got out between gasps of breath. Talking was definitely straining. It dawned on me that they had him hooked to a heart monitor. That's what I was hearing slowly beeping each time his heart beat.

"I love you too." Tears started rolling down my face. I already knew in my heart that this was going to be the last time I talked to my son. 'Oh God' my mind screamed.

"Today's.. my.. birthday.." Jeremy was gasping for breath, straining so hard to get the words out.

"I know, honey. Happy Birthday." My voice was soft, barely able to speak myself.

"I'm.. going.. to have.. a.. great party." I could hear his loud, labored breathing. The sound of his voice got softer with each word he spoke. Tears were rolling down my face.

"You are? What are you" I pursed my lips as I tried to get the words out. "What are you going to do?"

"I.. am.. going.. to party.. with Jesus.. tonight" was the last words I heard him say.

I heard Tess scream "Jeremy". The beeping sound had changed. It was now just a steady stream. The EMT was yelling for the driver to hurry, 'He's in d-fib! We're losing him!"

The phone was still on.. I sat there in bed, frozen as I listened to what was going on in the back of that ambulance. The EMT was talking loudly as he was trying to get Jeremy's heart started again. He kept saying "Hang in there! We're almost there Don't quit on me!"

More was a lot going on, but I really couldn't understand all that was being said. Tess was crying and yelling at Jeremy to wake up, not to leave her and the kids. I started crying harder sitting there, listening.

I couldn't move. I couldn't think. Then when I heard someone yell "let's get him in...' The phone finally, blissfully went dead. That's when I realized that they had reached the hospital

"Oh God, Oh God" I yelled rocking back and forth on the bed.

Mandy jumped up on the bed when she heard me scream. She didn't wait for any invitation.

I don't know how long I sat there with the phone to my ear, listening to nothing. I had to call Kyle and Nat. I had to let them know what had just happened.

I don't know how I did it but managed to find the speed dial number to make a call.

"Kyle" I said softly when he answered the phone, "you and Nat have to come immediately. I need you."

Chapter 20

"I am told that Kirsten has something she would like to say" the pastor announced. I came back to the present and my senses when Colin touched my hand. I looked around before realizing it was my turn to speak.

I rose to my feet and walked slowly up the steps to stand beside the pastor. He gave my clenched fists a squeeze before he went to sit down when I got there. I put one hand on either side of the stand to steady myself.

I cleared my throat and took a sip of water from the glass that was sitting there. "Thank you, everyone, for coming. This is not one of those occasions that we like or even want to attend. Yet, it is so necessary for us... to be able to say.. 'Good-bye' to someone we love and hold especially dear."

I had to pause to push back the tears fighting their way to the surface. I had to find my voice again.

Through a crackly voice I continued, "Some of you here today believe in God and know Him as your Savior. Some of you don't. But I want to tell you there is a God. He loves you and me no matter what. And He also gives us visions for our lives and the lives of our sons and our daughters."

I gulped. I knew I wasn't going to be able to keep the tears at bay for long. Hopefully, long enough.

"God blessed me such a vision for my children, many, many years ago" I was slow to speak. "He told me that my sons would serve him greatly. He told me one would be called to tell the world of his great love. Nathaniel speaks to everyone he meets about his faith in God."

I had to take a breath. "He told me one would minister to foreigners. Kyle has gone on many mission trips over the years providing his services to the needy."

This was the hard part. "And, one would be called home." I paused, taking another deep breath. Tears were stinging my eyes. "And that's where Jeremy is today. He demonstrated God's love each and every day with his devotion to his family." The tears were coming again. I could no longer hold them back. Did they ever really stop?

I really didn't know if I could be understood. I spoke slowly, and the crackling in my voice couldn't have made it easy for anyone. I just hoped I spoke loud enough for all to hear the words I had to say.

"I wanted to share this gift with you so you all could know. There is a loving God. And he is here with us now.

Today, at this very moment." I paused only slightly before continuing,

"He gives us hope and dreams to guide us throughout our lives. He gives us strength to endure hard times. He gives us comfort in our hour of need. He gives us peace throughout it all. For we are His children and His alone."

I closed my eyes, took a deep breath and opened my eyes again. I wiped the tears from my face and gathered what little composure I had before continuing again.

"I know God was there with Jeremy that night. He died knowing exactly where his spirit was going. He was going to rejoice in the presence of God. He was there then and he's here with us now, in our presence. He is always with us and always will be no matter what happens in our lives. And, by his good grace, we'll continue on."

I stopped talking. The tears finally overwhelming me. Sobs making it impossible to speak. Nat and Kyle grabbed one arm each to steady me as I swayed. They escorted me down the steps.

Colin was waiting there to take my hand. I looked up at him. Thru the tears I asked, "Is today the day you will accept Jesus?"

He answered softly, "Yes" then lead me back to my seat.

It was done. That was it. The most important thing that I had to do. There was nothing else I had to think or do today.

www.ingramcontent.com/pod-product-compliance
Lightning Source LLC
Chambersburg PA
CBHW031006210726
48290CB00007B/2495